The Birth

by Lois Podoshen

illustrations by Sally Schaedler

 Richard C. Owen Publishers, Inc.
Katonah, New York

I got a bird for my birthday.

But Mom said,
"I don't like birds in the house."

I showed her how he sat
on my finger.

But Mom said,
"I don't like birds in the house."

I put his cage
next to Mom's chair.

He spread his pretty feathers,
just for her.

He chirped a pretty song,
just for her.

I opened his cage.

He flew to Mom's finger.

"I don't like birds in the house,"
said Mom, "but I like you!"